To Angela, with love – R.E.
To Edward Winter, with love – S.W.

First published in Great Britain in 2005 and in the USA in 2006
by Frances Lincoln Children's Books, 4 Torriano Mews,
Torriano Avenue, London NW5 2RZ

www.franceslincoln.com

Distributed in the USA by Publishers Group West

British Library Cataloguing in Publication Data available on request

ISBN 10: 1-84507-291-X
ISBN 13: 978-1-84507-291-9

The illustrations are watercolour and crayon

Printed in China

3 5 7 9 8 6 4 2

Little Monkey's
One Safe Place

Richard Edwards
Illustrated by Susan Winter

F

FRANCES LINCOLN
CHILDREN'S BOOKS

Little Monkey was playing high up in the treetops.

He climbed

and he jumped.

He swung by his hands

and he swung by his feet.

All morning he played until, tired out,
he found a comfortable place in the branches
and curled up for a sleep.

But while Little Monkey was sleeping
a storm blew up and dark clouds
covered the sun. Lightning flashed,
thunder crashed and gusts of wind
shook Little Monkey awake.

He was scared by the storm, but he held
on tight to the tree and scrambled down
to the ground.

Then he ran home through the rain.

"I was afraid," said Little Monkey
to his mother.

She cuddled him.
"It's all right, Little Monkey.
You're safe now. Don't forget,
you've always got one safe place."
"Where?" asked Little Monkey.
"Don't you know?"
Little Monkey shook his head.
"Well, see if you can find it,"
said his mother.

So Little Monkey went looking for his one safe place.
First he ran to a hollow tree and climbed inside.

But a big green snake
came hissing and chased
Little Monkey away.

"That's not my one safe place,"
said Little Monkey.

He went down to the river
and splashed across to an island.

'Perhaps this is my one safe place,' he thought.

But a big green crocodile came snapping
and chased him back to the bank.

"That's not my one safe place,"
said Little Monkey.

Little Monkey searched all through the jungle for his one safe place.

At last he came to a
dark cave and peeped in.
Everything was quiet.

'Perhaps this is my one safe place,'
he thought, and he crept inside.

But suddenly he heard a growl and saw a pair of big green eyes glaring from the shadows.

Little Monkey jumped up and ran away as fast as he could.

Back through the forest he raced,
until he reached the clearing where
his mother was waiting.

"Well?" she asked. "Have you found
your one safe place?"

"No," said Little Monkey sadly.
"I looked in a tree, but that wasn't it.
I looked by the river, but that wasn't it.
I looked in a cave, but that wasn't it.
I don't think I'll ever find
my one safe place."
    And a tear trickled out of his eye.

"Come here," said Little Monkey's mother.
Little Monkey pressed forward against her
warm body. She closed her arms around him,
wrapping him up.

"This is your one safe place," she said.
"It's here. It's in my arms."
Little Monkey smiled and wriggled happily
as his mother hugged him.

At last he had found his
one safe place.